Clever Trap

For Ada, with love — L. F.

For my buddy, Antonio — M. P.

Barefoot Books
2067 Massachusetts Ave
Cambridge, MA 02140

First published in the United States of America by Barefoot Books, Inc in 2014

Graphic design by Katie Jennings Campbell, Asheville, NC, USA
and Barefoot Books, Oxford
Reproduction by B & P International, Hong Kong
Printed in China on 100% acid-free paper
This book was typeset in Bembo Infant, Liam and Pinto
The illustrations were prepared in acrylic paint and graphite on paper that is
produced in Sicily near Mount Etna

The editors would like to thank the children at Thameside Primary School,
Reading, UK for all their careful reading

Sources:
Paskin Carrison, Muriel. "The Story of Princess Amaradevi" in *Cambodian Folk Stories from the Gatiloke*. Charles E. Tuttle Company, Vermont, 1987.

ISBN 978-1-78285-103-5

Library of Congress Cataloging-in-Publication Data
is available under LCCN 2013031137

1 3 5 7 9 8 6 4 2

Dara's Clever Trap

A Story from Cambodia

Retold by Liz Flanagan

Illustrated by Martina Peluso

CONTENTS

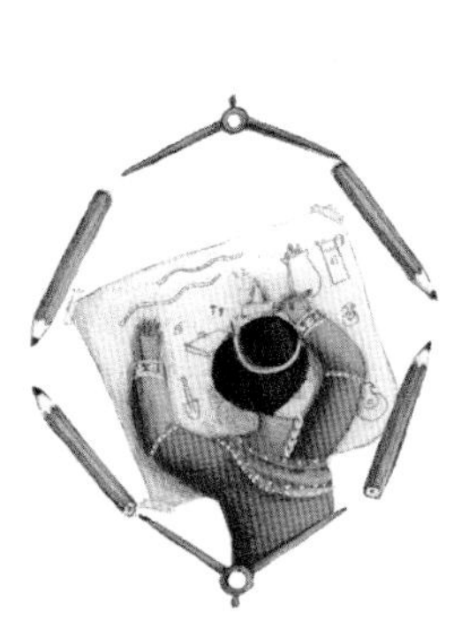

CHAPTER 1

Clever Dara

A long time ago, in the Kingdom of Cambodia, there was a rich and beautiful princess called Dara. She was clever and quick to learn many things.

Soon Dara was famous for her talents in music, writing and painting. Dara was also skilled in law, science and engineering. She loved to draw and build.

At the king's court, there was a young man called Rith who was also very skilled at planning and drawing.

When Dara saw Rith's beautiful plans she said, "Let's see which of us can design the most wonderful building!"

Dara and Rith worked all day and all night to finish their plans.

The king came to judge the competition. He named Dara as the winner.

Afterwards, Dara and Rith realized they had fallen in love. So Rith asked the king if he could marry Dara. The king agreed. He loved his daughter very much, and he wanted her to be happy.

Dara and Rith got married. They designed a beautiful palace to live in.

They filled it with lovely paintings and silk curtains and golden treasures. They built a workroom with enormous windows, two drawing boards and two huge chests to store all their drawings.

They spent their days living and working together. They built houses and bridges and temples. Soon they were very busy. Everyone came to them because their work was the best.

CHAPTER 2

The Wicked Ministers

The king had three ministers. Their job was to advise the king. But they were wicked and they did not like Rith because they were jealous of him. They wanted Dara's riches for themselves.

The ministers went to the king. They said, "Rith is planning to hurt you."

The king said, "Go away! I don't believe your lies. Rith is a good man."

One day Dara said to Rith, "Let's build a summer palace for my father. It will be a surprise for him because he has been so good to us. It will be the finest palace ever!"

Rith agreed. "Your father would love a cool and airy summer palace. Let's start straight away."

"If this is to be a palace unlike any other, we will need to build it with a special material," Dara said. "I will go to the mountains to look for white stone."

"I will miss you. Come home soon," Rith said as Dara set off.

The ministers saw that Dara had gone away. "Aha! Now is our chance!" they said. "While Dara's gone, let's get rid of Rith once and for all!"

One of them went to spy on Rith to see how he could get him into trouble with the king. He saw the plans for the king's summer palace. He stole the plans and wrote "King Rith's Palace" at the top.

Then the ministers took the plans to the king. "Rith wants to be king. He is planning to kill you," they lied. "Look, he is building a new palace for himself to live in once you are dead."

This time the king believed them. He was angry, and he sent Rith far away. He said Rith could never set foot inside Cambodia again.

CHAPTER 3

Dara's Plan

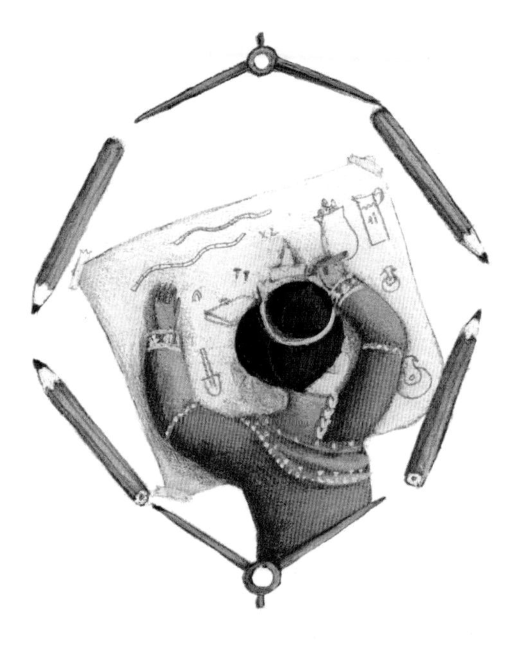

When Dara came home from her visit, she was very upset to hear what had happened.

She shut herself away in the palace she had built with Rith. She wept for her husband. Without Rith, Dara was sad and lonely.

But Dara knew she could not bring Rith back just by crying. So as she wept, she walked up and down in her beautiful empty palace, thinking and planning. She wanted to prove that Rith was a good and loyal man.

Meanwhile, the three evil ministers met and plotted together.

"We will take turns asking Dara to marry us," they said. "Whichever one of us she chooses, we will share her riches between us. Soon we will be wealthy!"

Dara was very clever and guessed what had happened. She knew the ministers had lied to her father. She dried her tears. She began to make a plan to bring Rith back.

The next morning, one minister came to Dara's palace. He told the princess, "You are the most beautiful woman in the whole world, and I have always loved you. Will you marry me?"

Dara decided to trick the minister. She knew that he didn't love her.

She said, "Why don't you return this evening at seven o'clock, and we can talk again about this?"

The very same morning, the second minister visited Dara in her palace. He also asked the princess to marry him.

Dara was surprised, but she said, "Come back this evening at eight o'clock."

Straight afterwards, the third minister came to Dara and asked her to marry him. She told him to return at nine o'clock.

Dara had a maid called Chenda who was clever and very good at noticing things, big and small.

Chenda said to Dara, "Just after you went on your journey, someone broke into your workroom. The plans for the king's summer palace have gone missing."

Dara said, "I think I know who stole them and why."

“Please get my drawing board ready.” Dara said to Chenda. “I have work to do!”

Chenda brought Dara’s tools. All morning Dara worked hard, planning and drawing.

Chenda brought food for Dara, but the princess did not stop to eat or drink until her work was done.

Clever Dara thought and drew. She sketched, and she tested. Finally she said, "There! I will build a trap to catch these wicked men."

Chapter 4

The Trap of Rice and Mud

Dara told her servants all about her plan.

"Build a big pit under this room," she said. She showed them her drawings so they knew what to do. She explained how to build the pit so the walls would be strong and would not cave in.

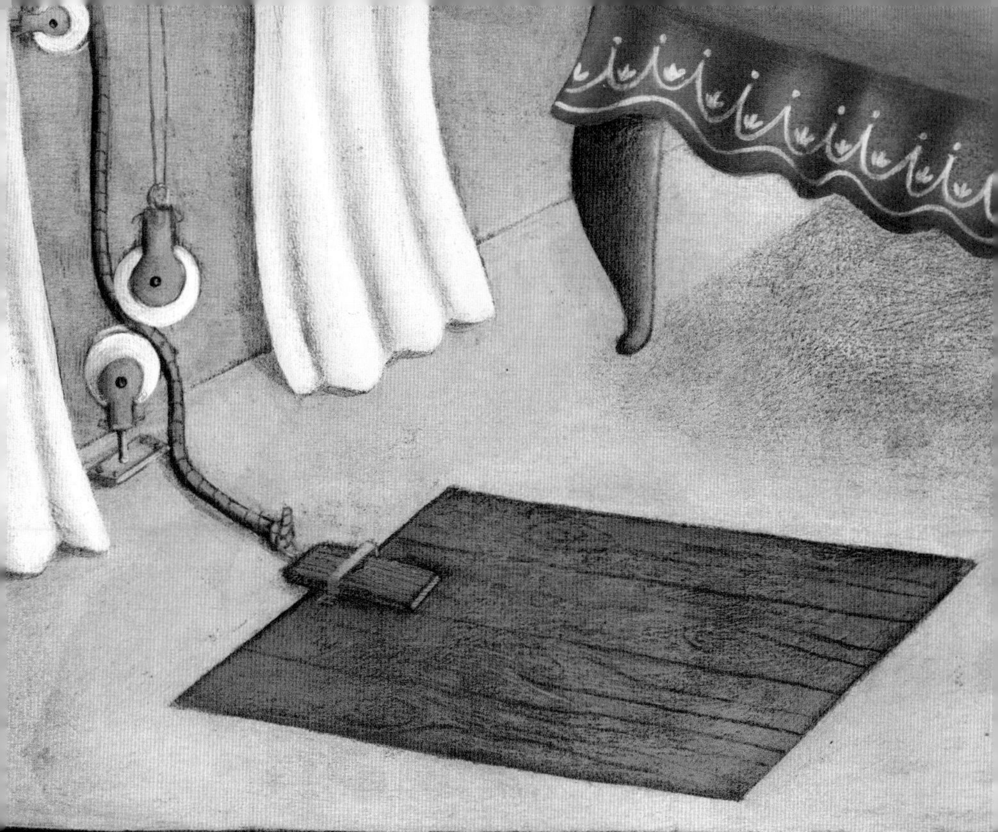

"Next, fill the pit with sticky rice, mud and hot water," the princess said. "Then cover it all with a trapdoor, like this. It will open with these ropes and pulleys."

Dara's servants worked all that long hot day to build the trap.

When they had finished, the princess tied a strong rope to the trapdoor and hid it behind some gold curtains.

Then she said to Chenda, "Bring all my most precious things and lay them on this table near the trapdoor."

Chenda smiled and did as the princess asked. She brought string, a ruler, a pencil and a spirit level. Then she brought an emerald ring, a ruby necklace, diamond bracelets and some pearl earrings.

The trap was complete.

At seven o'clock the first minister arrived at Dara's palace. Chenda welcomed him politely and took him to the room with the trap.

"Please wait here," Chenda said. "Princess Dara won't be long."

Then Dara and Chenda hid behind the gold curtains in the same room and watched the minister.

The greedy minister looked at the gleaming jewels on the table. He stretched out his hand to take one, but then pulled it back.

"I must not take anything. These jewels belong to Dara," he thought.

But he couldn't stop himself. At last, he reached out and stole the shining emerald ring. He stuffed it deep in his pocket. "Dara doesn't care about jewels anyway," he muttered.

Dara nodded to Chenda. They both pulled hard on the rope.

The trapdoor opened wide. The ropes and pulleys all worked perfectly. The minister fell into the pit of warm, sticky rice and mud. Plop! He landed right on the top.

The trapdoor sprang shut,

trapping him inside.

"Help!" he cried. "I'm stuck!"

But nobody could hear him.

The next minister arrived at eight o' clock. Chenda showed him into the room.

This man stole the shimmering ruby necklace and put it in his pocket.

Just as before, Dara and Chenda pulled the rope and the minister was caught in the trap.

At nine o'clock the last minister arrived. He grabbed a glittering diamond bracelet and hid it in his pocket.

Whoosh! Down went the trapdoor. Down went the minister. Plop! He landed on the pile of rice and mud below.

Chapter 5

The Proof

Dara left the three wicked ministers in the trap of rice and mud all night long.

The ministers were sticky, muddy and damp, but they came to no harm.

The next morning, Dara said to her servants, "Take the ministers out of the pit. Tie their hands and bring them to my father's court."

Then Dara put on her best robes and went to see the king.

In front of all the fine people of the court, Dara bowed low to her father.

She said, “Please let me prove to you that Rith is innocent. I can show you that your ministers are wicked and greedy.”

Everybody gasped in surprise.

The king was shocked, but he trusted Dara. "Please tell me the truth," he said.

Dara clapped her hands, and her servants brought in the three ministers. They were wet and covered in mud and rice.

Everybody laughed and pointed at them.

"These men are liars," Dara said. "They wanted you to send Rith away, so one of them could marry me and take my riches."

The king said, "These are serious words. Can you prove it to me?"

"Yes, I can prove it," Dara said. "These men said they loved me, but they only love my jewels. Look!"

Chenda reached into the first minister's pocket and took out the emerald ring.

"He stole my ring," Dara said. "And then I caught him in a trap."

Next, Chenda took the ruby necklace and the diamond bracelet from the other two men.

"They have stolen my jewels, but that isn't all," Dara explained. "We were planning to build you a summer palace as a surprise. They stole the plans and lied to you about them. Rith did not want to be king, and the palace was not for us — it was for you!"

When he heard that, the king wept and asked his daughter to forgive him. "I'm sorry for believing the ministers. I was wrong, Dara. Your husband Rith is innocent."

Dara forgave her father. Then she sent the fastest messenger in the land to bring Rith home again.

The king was very angry with his lying ministers. "Take them around my whole kingdom," he said. "Everyone must hear what they have done."

The ministers were tied to three elephants and taken away.

The next day, Rith came home to his wife. Dara ran out to meet him.

They lived together for the rest of their days. They built the summer palace for the king, and he was delighted with it. When the king died, Dara and Rith ruled together. They were always remembered for the beauty of their designs, the strength of their love and the cleverness of brave Princess Dara.